The Mountains of Tibet

LIBRARY
DICKMAN ELEMENTARY SCHOOL

The Mountains of Tibet

MORDICAI GERSTEIN

Harper & Row, Publishers

The Mountains of Tibet
Copyright © 1987 by Mordicai Gerstein
Printed in the U.S.A. All rights reserved.
1   2   3   4   5   6   7   8   9   10
First Edition

Library of Congress Cataloging-in-Publication Data
Gerstein, Mordicai.
    The Mountains of Tibet.

    Summary: After dying, a Tibetan woodcutter is given
the choice of going to heaven or living another life
anywhere in the universe.
    [1. Reincarnation—Fiction.   2. Tibet (China)—
Fiction]   I. Title.
PZ7.G325Mo 1987   [E]   85-45684
ISBN 0-06-022144-5
ISBN 0-06-022149-6 (lib. bdg.)

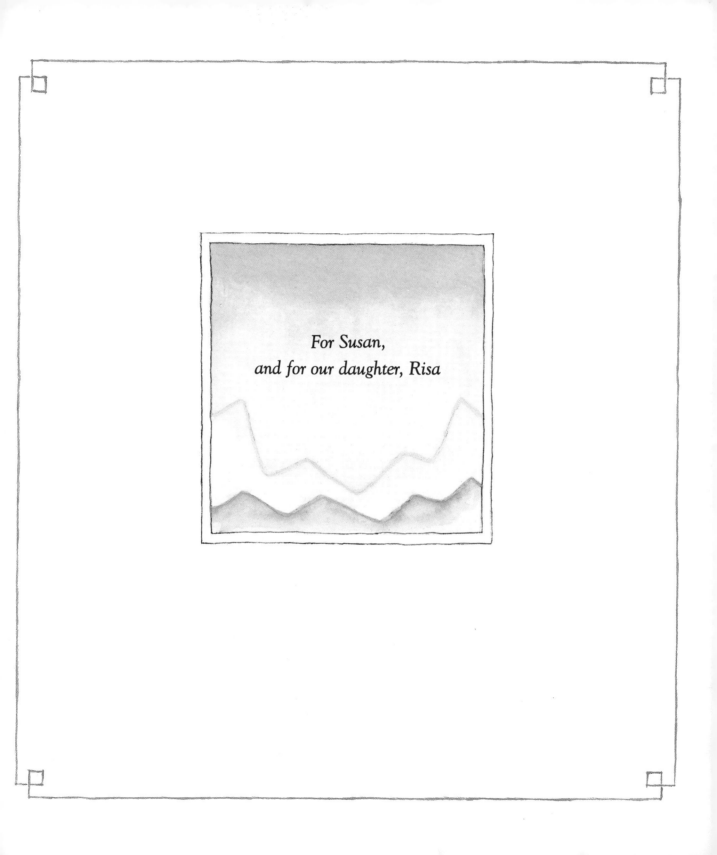

For Susan,
and for our daughter, Risa

In a tiny village, in a valley, high in the mountains
of Tibet, a little boy was born. He loved to fly kites.

On clear nights he liked to look up at the Milky Way
and the stars.

"There are other worlds up there," he said to himself.
"Someday I'm going to visit them."

He grew up to be a woodcutter. As he gathered his wood, he looked out beyond the far mountains.

"There are other countries out there," he said to himself, "cities and oceans, and people of other races. Someday I'll go and see them."

But he was always busy with his work and his wife
and children.

He lived to be very old, and he never left his valley.

Then he died.

He found himself in a place that was both very dark and very bright. He heard a voice speaking to him. The voice said:

"You now have a
choice. You may become
part of the endless universe some
call heaven, or you may live another life."
"I want to live another life," said the woodcutter.
"The one I just lived has faded from my mind
like a dream. All I can remember is that
I wanted to see more of the world."
"Look around you,"
said the voice.

The woodcutter looked out and saw all the worlds of the universe. They blazed and spun like fireworks on New Year's Eve.

"There are hundreds of millions of worlds," said the voice. "They are called galaxies. Each one is different and each one is beautiful, and you may choose any one you like to live in."

Then the woodcutter heard the galaxies singing to him.

"Choose me! Choose me!" sang each one. The woodcutter was frightened; his head began to spin.

"How can I choose?" he cried.

"Choose from your heart," the voice replied.

There was a pinwheel-shaped galaxy that looked like a great splash of milk.

"I like that one," said the woodcutter.

"That galaxy has hundreds of millions of stars," said the voice. "They come in all shapes and sizes, and any one you like may be your own."

All the stars of the galaxy sparkled for the woodcutter. They flashed like fireflies in the woods on a summer night. But one star caught his eye. Its light was warm and golden.

"I'll take that one," said the woodcutter.

"That star," said the voice, "has nine perfect planets revolving around it. Which one would you like to be your home?"

The woodcutter saw the nine planets, each in its place.

One was huge with swirling clouds. Another was red. One had sparkling rings around it and many moons. One looked like a blue-green marble the woodcutter had had long ago as a boy.

"I like that one," said the woodcutter. "Somehow it looks like home."

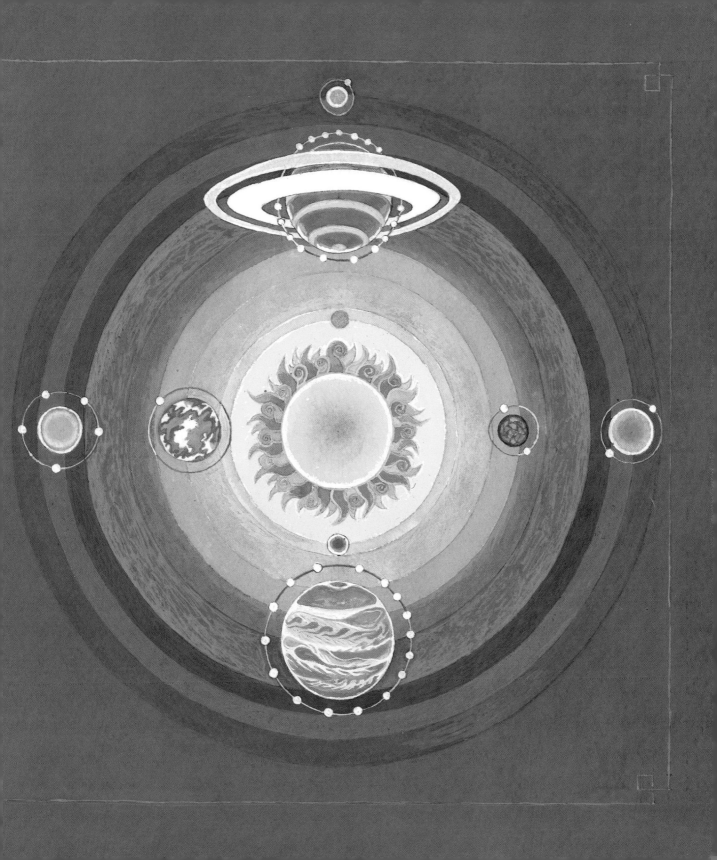

"On that planet," said the voice, "live hundreds of thousands of different and wonderful creatures. You may live your life as any one you like. Which will you be?"

The woodcutter looked again, and there were all the different creatures parading past him. Some swam, some danced, and some flew.

"Come be like me!" each one called. "See how much fun you'll have! See how beautiful you'll be!"

There were whales and goldfish, lions and pussycats. There were snakes and giraffes. There were butterflies, and there were people. The woodcutter almost decided to be a sea gull gliding on the sea breeze. Then he saw a child watching the sea gull and laughing. The child was flying a kite.

"I want to be a person," said the woodcutter.

"There are thousands of kinds of people in this world," said the voice. "Each with different dances and delicious dishes, and you may join any kind you like!"

The woodcutter looked and saw all the peoples of the world dancing around him. They looked like flowers.

There were red, white, and golden people. There were black, brown, and pink people. Some wore feathers and some wore silks. Some wore plaids, some stripes. They all danced their dances and called to him in all their different languages.

"Just taste this!" they called, holding out their most tempting dishes.

"This is the hardest choice," said the woodcutter.

Finally, the music of the golden people touched his heart.

"I will join them," he said.

"Now," said the voice, "where on your planet would you like to be born? It may be anywhere you like."

Then the woodcutter saw all the countries that he'd never seen during his life. He saw forests and plains, he saw deserts and green islands. He saw great cities and lush jungles, but there was one green valley, high in the craggy mountains, that seemed to wink at him and whisper old familiar stories.

"That looks like a perfect place to be born," said the woodcutter.

"There are dozens of young mothers and fathers in that valley," said the voice. "Whichever you like best will be yours."

The woodcutter felt the love of all the young mothers and fathers of the valley flow up to him.

They all smiled and held out their arms to him calling: "Come to us! Come be ours!"

He saw a man whose smile made his heart sing. He saw a woman whose smile made him feel safe and warm.

"I want them for my parents," he said.

"Last," said the voice, "you may choose whether to be a boy or a girl."

"I seem to remember that I was a boy," said the woodcutter. "This time I'd like to see what being a girl is like."

And so, in a tiny village, in a valley, high in the
mountains of Tibet, a little girl was born. She loved
to fly kites.

THE MOUNTAINS OF TIBET grew out of Mordicai Gerstein's reading of the Tibetan Book of the Dead. The illustrations were done on Arches watercolor paper with watercolor and gouache.

Mordicai Gerstein was born in Los Angeles, lived for over twenty-five years in New York City, and now resides with his wife and daughter in western Massachusetts. He has been a painter, a sculptor, a director of animation, and a filmmaker.

Mr. Gerstein has written and illustrated many children's books, including ARNOLD OF THE DUCKS, a *School Library Journal* Best Book of Spring 1983; THE ROOM; and most recently, TALES OF PAN.

E   Gerstein, Mordicai
G

The mountains of
Tibet

$11.89

DATE			

LIBRARY
SHERMAN ELEMENTARY SCHOOL

© THE BAKER & TAYLOR CO.